Tears of Joy

Fifty percent of the profits from this book will be used to educate children about childhood sexual abuse.

Thank you Ellen Anderson, Janine Arseneau, Susan Ashley, Diana Dempster, Ani DiFranco, Janis Ian, Karen Knutson, Diane Laska, Dr. Lois Lee, Elizabeth Mancosky, Barbara Stutz, and Marilyn Van Derbur.

Barbara J. Behm has been an author and editor of published children's books since 1986. Her four dogs keep her amused and entertained. Ellen Anderson joyfully shares her life with her husband, three children, three cats, and a parakeet. She has illustrated five other children's books, and her colorful greeting cards from Ellen Anderson Illustrations are available in stores nationwide.

For Lynn, Margaret, and Beverly, and all the children of the world, courageously growing up. B. B.
For all children and those who care about them. E. A.

Library of Congress Catalog Card Number 98-91062
ISBN 0-9669647-0-5

To receive a copy of this book, send a check or money order for $16.95 plus $3 shipping to WayWord Publishing, P. O. Box 522, Thiensville, WI 53092. Wisconsin residents add 5% sales tax. Discounts given for multiple copies. Visit WayWord Publishing on the web at www.execpc.com/~wayword/
E-mail: wayword@execpc.com

Printed in the United States of America

1 2 3 4 5 6 7 8 9 04 03 02 01 99

WayWord
Publishing

Carly was born a beautiful baby girl...healthy and happy and loving all the world. As she grew, she played with toys, laughed a lot, read a great many books, and had probably the largest stuffed animal collection ever gathered!

As she grew some more, Carly's world became even better. If that were possible! There were so many places to discover, friends to make, and things to grow up to be.

Carly loved her family, her friends, her teachers, and all her stuffed animals. Carly often shouted for joy just because she loved all the world!

But one day, Carly suddenly was silent and sad. She did not want to play with her toys or read her books. She placed all her stuffed animals around the edges of her bed so they would protect her from all the world and keep all the world — AWAY!

Carly cried and cried into the fur of all her
animal friends — the only friends she
thought she truly had. They were all
very concerned.

Carly stopped talking to her family
and friends and teachers.

She didn't play anymore.
She did not even go outside.

She just wanted to stay in her
room to be comforted by the
sweet-eyed animals.

Carly no longer laughed.

She was not the same
cheerful child as before.

Weeks went by. Carly's mother and
brother tried to talk to her. Carly would
not talk. Carly's teacher tried to talk to
her. Carly would not talk. Carly's best
friend, Lily, tried to talk to her. Carly
would not talk. Carly had changed.

Then one day at school,
Carly's teacher gently took
her by the hand and led her
into Miss Mitchell's office.
Carly sat on a couch next to
Miss Mitchell, the counselor
at Carly's school. Carly was
scared to be there at first,
but Miss Mitchell had
probably the second largest
stuffed animal collection
ever gathered!

After a little bit of her shyness left her, Carly hugged a brown, furry bear; a soft, yellow goose; a black-and-white spotted dog with a bright red tongue; a chubby, pink pig; and a giraffe whose neck nearly went through the ceiling!

Soon Carly was hugging so many animals that
when she sat back, she completely disappeared!
Miss Mitchell started to giggle and then
laughed real hard. And for the first time in
a very, very long time...so did Carly.

When everyone returned to their places,
Miss Mitchell asked Carly why she had been
feeling so sad. Carly turned away and would not
answer. Then Miss Mitchell put a puppet over
her hand. It was a soft, brown puppet of a horse.

Miss Mitchell used a make-believe voice to pretend it was the horse doing the talking. The horse said, "Hello, Carly. You can talk to me. You can trust me... with anything. Please tell me what is wrong. Don't be sad...forever."

Carly smiled slightly because it was funny to see the horse talking and, at the same time, know that it was really Miss Mitchell who was actually doing the talking. It made Carly feel better to know that someone would be so kind to her.

The horse asked Carly, "Why have you been so unhappy, my little friend?" Carly looked away and became very withdrawn. The horse said, "Don't worry. No one will hurt you. You are safe with me."

Carly gasped and let out a big sigh as tears quietly flowed down her cheeks. The soft, brown horse gently wiped the tears from Carly's face.

Carly reached for the horse and held it in her arms and cried into its fur. Carly said, "Someone has been touching me in a bad way ... in my private parts. He told me not to tell!" Then Carly cried and cried, holding onto the horse and Miss Mitchell for dear life. She cried and cried until she got all her tears out.

Miss Mitchell told Carly that she was very brave to tell. She said that it is important to try to talk about things whenever she feels sad or scared. Carly realized that keeping secrets only makes things worse. Miss Mitchell told Carly that she had done exactly the right thing. She said that children who feel sad or scared should talk and keep talking until they find someone who will listen...and understand...and believe what they are saying.

The animals all leaned forward and listened very closely.

Miss Mitchell said, "If your family does not want to hear you, tell your best friend's mom. If she does not want to hear you, tell your teachers. If they do not want to hear you, tell the nurse or counselor at school. Keep telling your story until someone listens and believes."

Miss Mitchell told Carly that the bad and confusing touching was not Carly's fault. She promised to find some help for the family. Miss Mitchell assured Carly that she would do everything possible to keep her safe.

Carly felt so much better. Miss Mitchell hugged her good-bye. As Carly was leaving, Miss Mitchell said in a make-believe voice, "Hey, don't forget me!" Then she handed the horse to Carly as a gift. This time, Carly's tears were tears of joy.

Childhood Sexual Abuse

What Is Childhood Sexual Abuse?
Childhood sexual abuse is the exploitation of a child for the sexual gratification of an abuser.

It includes any of the following:
- The touching of a child's private parts. (Private parts are any areas of the body covered by a bathing suit.)
- Discussion of sexual topics with a child for sexual gratification.
- Exposure of the child's or abuser's private parts.
- Taking photographs or filming video of a child's private parts.
- Forced observation of sexual acts or pornographic photos or films.
- Any sexual acts involving touching, fondling, penetration, exhibitionism, oral sex, or intercourse.
- Any sexual contact between an adult and a child.

How To Stop It
Take time to talk with and listen to your children in depth every single day. Know what activities they are involved in and with whom. Know who your children are chatting with on the computer and what they are chatting about. Make sure your telephone number and address are never revealed on-line. Be on the alert if a child feels unsafe or uncomfortable with, or dreads spending time with, a certain individual. If you suspect that abuse has occurred, encourage the child to talk about it. Give emotional support when she or he does talk.

Teach children that their bodies belong to *only* them and that no one has the right to touch them in a bad or confusing way on any part of their bodies. Teach children how to say *NO* to the abuser and to get away from the situation and the abuser...and to tell somebody they trust about it until they are believed and action is taken.

Although ninety percent of children know their abuser, strangers can and do abuse children. Help children understand the dangers posed by adults who use child-luring tactics, such as searching for a nonexistent lost pet or the offer of toys, candy, or money. Teach children that they should never go anywhere without telling you where and with whom. Trust your own instincts. If you feel someone should not be around the child, limit the person's access.

If Abuse Occurs

If abuse occurs and a child shares her or his story about it, stay calm and listen to the child carefully.

Believe the child. Children rarely lie about sexual abuse. Tell the child that he or she is very brave and did the right thing to tell somebody.

Get professional assistance, counseling, and medical care by calling your county's social services/child protection/child welfare agency. Agency numbers can be found in the telephone book in the county governmental listings.

Above all, love and emotionally support the child. Your love and support cannot undo the abuse, but they will go a long way in helping the child recover and heal.

Tell the child that the abuse is not her or his fault. It is **NEVER** the child's fault.

To stop the abuse, we must start talking

Sexual abuse of children is one of the last great taboos of our society, and *it must stop*. To protect our children, we must teach them how to recognize it, how to say no to it, and how to seek help if it does occur. We must teach our children to tell the secrets their abusers manipulated them into keeping; and we must be willing to listen, believe, and take action to hold abusers accountable.

Sexual abuse of children is prevalent beyond the wildest imagination. The shocking statistics reveal that one of four girls and one of nine boys are sexually abused before the age of seventeen. The average age of the child for the first incident is six. Ninety percent of the children know their abuser, who is often a trusted adult who "grooms" the child over time. Sexual abuse of children occurs in every ethnic, social, and economic category.

Besides the trauma, shame, and elimination of joy that sexual abuse can cause a child, the repercussions of the abuse often carry over into adulthood. Just one incident in childhood can lead to a lifetime of anxiety, depression, isolation, fear, self-destructive behaviors, aggression, violence, sleep disorders, lack of confidence, criminal activity, eating disorders, alcohol and drug abuse, denial, alienation, low self-esteem, trust and intimacy problems, lack of emotional growth, and feelings of guilt and worthlessness — especially if the child victim does not tell anyone about the abuse or tries to tell but is not believed.

Children are targeted for sexual abuse because they are usually smaller, easier to manipulate, physically weaker, and vulnerable when compared to adults. Therefore, it is up to all of us as caring, protective adults to empower ourselves to recognize and put a stop to sexual abuse. We must also empower our children and encourage them to talk to us — about everything.